Thayer Memorial Library

P.O. Box 5 ✦ 717 Main Street ✦ Lancaster, Massachusetts 01523 ✦ (978)368-8928 ✦ Fax (978)368-8929

BATMAN™

POISON IVY'S SCARE FAIR

by
Donald Lemke

illustrated by
Andie Tong

Batman created by
Bob Kane with Bill Finger

HARPER FESTIVAL
An Imprint of HarperCollinsPublishers

HarperFestival is an imprint of HarperCollins Publishers.

Batman: Poison Ivy's Scare Fair
Copyright © 2017 DC Comics.
BATMAN and all related characters and elements © & ™ DC Comics. The DC LOGO: ™ & © DC.
(s17)

HARP36458
Manufactured in China.

Library of Congress Control Number: 2016939290
ISBN 978-0-06-236077-9

Book design by Victor Joseph Ochoa and Erica De Chavez
16 17 18 19 20 SCP 10 9 8 7 6 5 4 3 2 1

❖ First Edition

BATMAN

Orphaned as a child, young Bruce Wayne trained his body and mind to become Batman, the Dark Knight. He is an expert martial artist, crime fighter, and detective. Using high-tech gadgets and weapons, Batman fights against the most dangerous criminals in Gotham City.

BATGIRL

Barbara Gordon fights alongside Batman, using high-tech gadgets and martial arts skills. Her father, James Gordon, does not know her secret identity as Batgirl.

COMMISSIONER JAMES GORDON

James Gordon is the Gotham City Police Commissioner. He works with Batman to stop crime in the city.

POISON IVY

Poison Ivy, also known as Pamela Isley, is a former scientist. The super-villain has the power to control plants. She'll stop at nothing to protect the world's plant life.

On the last weekend of summer, the gates of the county fair swing open. Thousands of people flood inside for rickety rides, blue ribbon bake-offs, and fried foods.

Even the city's two mayoral candidates arrive to shake hands and kiss babies. They will take part in the day's main event: world-record vegetables.

The candidates stand next to giant fruits and vegetables.
"Welcome, fairgoers!" one candidate says to the excited crowd.
The other holds up a large blue ribbon. "It's time to award today's
big winner!" she jokes.

Suddenly, the prize-winning pumpkin starts to tremble. The stage shakes. *Crack!* The pumpkin splits open, and out steps . . . Poison Ivy!

Fairgoers scream and scramble for the exits. "Do not fear me," Poison Ivy shouts. "These mutant fruits and vegetables are what you should fear!"

Poison Ivy lifts her arms toward the sky. At her command, the vines of a tomato plant grow and slither through the crowd like snakes. The vines twist around the candidates, who are trapped in a thick, leafy web.

Police Commissioner James Gordon is among the crowd of fairgoers.
"Wait here, Barbara," he tells his daughter. Then he heads for Poison Ivy.

A bushel of apples spills at the commissioner's feet. They burst open. The seeds grow into angry saplings, wrapping around Gordon and lifting him into the air.

"I'm not a fan of fair food," says Poison Ivy, "but a commissioner-on-a-stick looks pretty good!"

Meanwhile, Barbara sneaks away from the crowd and uses a hidden device to signal her super hero friend Batman. She is no ordinary teenager, after all. Barbara is secretly Batgirl!

Moments later, Batman arrives. The county fair is overrun with Poison Ivy's powerful plant life.

"Where do we begin?" Batgirl asks the super hero.

"Let's get to the root of the problem," says the Dark Knight.

The super heroes each remove a razor-sharp Batarang from their Utility Belts. *Fwip! Fwip!* They slice and dice their way through the vines until they reach the villain.

"What's eating you this time, Ivy?" Batman shouts.

"It's not what's eating me," the villain replies. "It's what this city is eating!" Poison Ivy points at the two captive candidates. "When *they* end the use of chemicals on our local crops, then I'll stop. The chemicals are ruining my vegetables!"

Poison Ivy's giant pumpkin is a trap. *Wham!* It snaps closed around Batman and Batgirl. The pumpkin's vine grows and grows, lifting the heroes a hundred feet into the air.

"Do you know what pumpkins always get me excited for?" Poison Ivy asks, watching the giant vegetable rise. "The fall."

Snap! The vine breaks, and the pumpkin plummets toward the ground.

Inside the pumpkin, Batman removes a Batarang from his Utility Belt. He shows the weapon to Batgirl, who smiles and nods. "Bombs away!" she says.

The Dark Knight flicks the Batarang, and the razor-sharp weapon sticks to the fleshy walls of the pumpkin. The super heroes quickly cover themselves with their fireproof capes.

Ka-boom! The pumpkin explodes, and a thousand charred pieces flutter down to the crowd below. Batman and Batgirl float to the ground on their outstretched capes.

The super heroes surround Poison Ivy and quickly place her in Bat-Cuffs. Her powerful plants wilt, releasing their captives.

"Violence doesn't get people to change," Batman tells Poison Ivy.
"Maybe not," she says, "But at least I've planted the seed."
As Gordon approaches, Batgirl hauls Poison Ivy away to
Arkham Asylum.

"Now what about this mess?" Batman asks.

"Oh, I wouldn't worry. Who would pass up a free snack at the fair?" says Gordon.

He picks up a piece of pumpkin and takes a bite. The two candidates do the same.

"Blech!" All three quickly spit out the flavorless food.
"Ivy may be on the wrong side of the law," says Batman,
smiling. "But when it comes to plants, she's usually right."